Poké Rap

I want to be the very best there ever was
To beat all the rest, yeah, that's my cause

Catch 'em, Catch 'em, Gotta catch 'em all

Pokémon I'll search across the land
Look far and wide
Release from my hand
The power that's inside

Catch 'em, Catch 'em, Gotta catch 'em all Pokémon!

Gotta catch 'em all, Gotta catch 'em all
Gotta catch 'em all, Gotta catch 'em all

At least one hundred and fifty or more to see
To be a Pokémon Master is my destiny

Catch 'em, Catch 'em, Gotta catch 'em all
Gotta catch 'em all, Pokémon! (repeat three times)

Can YOU Rap all 150?

**Here's the first 32 Pokémon.
Catch the next book *Ash to the Rescue*
for more of the Poké Rap.**

**Electrode, Diglett, Nidoran, Mankey
Venusaur, Rattata, Fearow, Pidgey
Seaking, Jolteon, Dragonite, Gastly
Ponyta, Vaporeon, Poliwrath, Butterfree**

**Venomoth, Poliwag, Nidorino, Golduck
Ivysaur, Grimer, Victreebel, Moltres
Nidoking, Farfetch'd, Abra, Jigglypuff
Kingler, Rhyhorn, Clefable, Wigglytuff**

Words and Music by Tamara Loeffler and John Siegler
Copyright © 1999 Pikachu Music (BMI)
Worldwide rights for Pikachu Music administered by Cherry River Music Co. (BMI)
All Rights Reserved   Used by Permission

Collect them all!

All Fired Up

All rights reserved. Published by Scholastic Inc., *Publishers since 1920*. SCHOLASTIC and associated logos are trademarks and/or registered trademarks of Scholastic Inc.

The publisher does not have any control over and does not assume any responsibility for author or third-party websites or their content.

ISBN 978-1-338-28409-6

10 9 8 7 6 5 4 3 2 1   18 19 20 21 22

Printed in the U.S.A.   40
First printing 2018

All Fired Up

Adapted by Jennifer Johnson

Scholastic Inc.

1

The Charicific Valley

"I have fought so many battles here in the Johto region," Ash Ketchum complained. "And I've only won one badge!"

Ash and his friends Misty and Brock were hiking through a mountain range. Ash, a young Pokémon Trainer, had come to the western territories on an errand for his mentor, Professor Oak. But it was Ash's lifelong dream to become the world's greatest Pokémon Master. So while he was here, he planned on earning badges from the gyms in the Johto League. Once he earned eight badges, he would compete in the Johto League Tournament.

So far, Ash was not having much luck. The Violet Gym was the only place Ash had won a badge.

Misty was another Pokémon Trainer. She had orange hair and specialized in Water-type Pokémon. She always carried around Togepi, a cute little Fairy-type Pokémon.

"You have fought a lot of battles here, Ash," Misty said. "But you can't expect to win badges when practically all your battles are against Team Rocket."

Team Rocket was a team of Pokémon thieves. Jessie, James, and Meowth were always trying to steal Pikachu. But they were even more well known for goofing up than for actually stealing any Pokémon.

"Of course," Misty went on, "it wouldn't mean much if they gave out badges for beating *those* pathetic thieves."

"You said it," Brock chimed in. Brock was a Pokémon breeder. He had once been the leader of his own gym.

Ash was beginning to feel insulted. "But Team Rocket isn't the only one I can beat in Pokémon battles," he pointed out. "Not with Pikachu by my side. And when things get really tough, I know Charizard will always help me out, too."

"*Pika!*" As usual, Ash's Electric-type Pokémon was perched right on top of Ash's red-and-white baseball cap. Ash could tell that the little yellow Pokémon agreed with him.

But Brock and Misty were another story. "When the going gets tough," Brock teased, "the tough get Charizard."

"Relying on Charizard all the time really isn't fair to your opponents," Misty added.

"Not fair?" Ash had trained a cute little Charmander and evolved it into Charmeleon and then into a flying, fire-breathing Charizard.

But Brock agreed with Misty. "Your average Pokémon wouldn't have a chance against Charizard," he pointed out.

"No way!" Ash said.

Suddenly, a voice came from somewhere in the mountains. "No way!" it shouted.

"What?" Ash looked all around but saw no one. "Did

you hear that?" he asked.

"That was just an echo," Brock assured him. "Listen — I'll yell 'hello' and it'll answer back." Brock cupped his hands around his mouth. "Hello!" he shouted, in goofy voice.

"Hello!" Brock's voice echoed back.

"Not bad," said a woman's voice. Ash and his friends looked up, startled. A tall woman stood on a ledge in front of them. The woman had spiky green hair. She wore pointy earrings, high leather boots, and red shorts with a matching top.

"Not bad at all," the woman repeated. "But if you want to hear a really great echo, you should try yelling 'Charizard.' You're near the Charicific Valley, after all."

Brock grabbed a guidebook from his backpack. He read out loud, "'The Charicific Valley Nature Reserve is a well-known Charizard habitat.'"

"That's right," the green-haired woman said. "I'm Liza. I'm a Charizard Trainer."

2

Charizard's Flight

"A Charizard Trainer!" Ash exclaimed. He was always happy to meet a fellow Pokémon Trainer – particularly one who specialized in Pokémon as cool as Charizard.

Liza leaned toward Ash. "You have a Charizard, too, don't you?"

"How did you know?" Ash asked.

Liza sniffed. "I can smell the scent of Charizard on your clothes," she said. "I've been waiting for you since I heard that a Trainer with a Charizard had won a badge at the Violet Gym. Would you like to come with me to see the Charicific Valley? I can tell you guys really love Pokémon."

"A natural Charizard habitat, huh?" Ash asked. "I'd definitely like to see that."

"Okay, then," Liza agreed. She raised her right arm and waved her walking stick in the air. "Come, Charla!" she shouted.

At that, an enormous Charizard came flying over the mountain peaks. Like all Charizard, Charla had wings, red-orange skin, and a tail with a flame on the end. But this Charizard had a pink bow on its head and a small hot-air balloon lashed to its tail. It landed on the path beside Ash and the others.

"This is Charla, my Charizard," Liza said.

Liza climbed aboard Charla's back. She pointed to Misty. "You and Brock can ride in the balloon basket."

"Hey, what about me?" Ash asked.

"There's only room for two in the basket," Liza explained. "You can follow on your own Charizard. Let's go!" Charla flapped its wings and took off.

Ash didn't get it. His Charizard was really strong and a great flyer. But it had never given him a ride. He'd better ask Liza before she disappeared. "You want me to ride on my Charizard's back?" he shouted.

Charla paused in the air. Liza stared coolly at Ash. "You're Charizard's Trainer, right? What kind of Trainer can't ride his Charizard?"

Ash felt insulted. "Of course I can!"

Ash fished a Poké Ball from his backpack. "All right, Charizard, I choose you!"

The Pokémon appeared with a mighty roar. Nervously, Ash walked up to it. "Charizard, can you fly with me on your back?"

Charizard looked shocked. It squeezed its eyes shut and shook its head back and forth.

Liza looked down at Ash and Charizard. "What's the matter, Charizard? Is Ash too heavy for you?"

Charizard was a stubborn Pokémon. Liza's words were all it took to change its mind. It turned around and motioned for Ash to climb onto its back. Ash and Pikachu tried to steady themselves as Charizard jolted up into the air.

Ash looked at his friends with envy. Liza's Charizard clearly knew how to carry passengers. Charla was cruising along smoothly.

Meanwhile, Ash's Charizard was giving him and Pikachu a very bumpy ride! It kept bobbing up and down and zooming wildly from side to side.

Liza gave Ash a funny look. "Follow me!" she shouted. Her Charla sped away, leaving Charizard behind.

Ash wasn't about to stand for that. He pumped his fist in the air. "Go, Charizard!"

His Pokémon began racing after Charla. Suddenly, it stopped dead in its tracks. A steep rock face loomed up ahead.

"Charizard! What are you doing?" Ash asked.

Charizard stopped so quickly that it forgot to fly at all. It plummeted toward the ground. Ash and Pikachu tumbled after it.

"Charizard!" Ash yelled again. Just in time, the Pokémon remembered to flap its wings. It rose up under Ash and Pikachu. They landed on Charizard's back.

"That's it! Steady now!" Ash told Charizard.

By now, they were near the bottom of a narrow gorge. Ash was afraid that Charizard would smash into

the sides. Or maybe it would plunge into the river that raged beneath them.

Charizard made it through the gorge, but Ash's troubles weren't over. A dense forest lay ahead of them.

"Hey, hey! Hold it! Wait! Charizard!" Ash screamed. Ash was sure that Charizard was going to fly into a tree.

By this time, Ash didn't even care about catching up with Liza. He just wanted to get to the valley in one piece. If Charizard didn't slow down, that wasn't going to happen!

Meanwhile, Liza and the others were already in the Charicific Valley. It wasn't hard to recognize. There were giant stone Charizard statues everywhere.

"The Charizard that live here are raised naturally, in the wild," Liza said.

"Raised naturally?" Misty asked.

"That's right," Liza told her. "In this valley, Charizard don't rely on human Trainers to help them become stronger. Instead, the Charizard compete against one another. It's intense training. The Charizard here are the strongest in the world."

Brock nodded his head. "I see," he said. "They all have the same goal, so they encourage one another. They grow strong together."

"That sounds a bit too hard for Ash's Charizard," Misty pointed out.

"Maybe so," Liza agreed. "It can't even keep up with my Charla."

"We kept up!" Ash protested. He and Charizard had arrived in the valley. They were just in time to hear Liza's insulting remark.

"Ash?" Misty and the others turned to stare at him and Charizard. The big Pokémon was panting and sweating. It had made the last leg of the trip on foot, with Ash and Pikachu still on its back.

"My Charizard made it," Ash repeated. "Even if it

couldn't fly here."

Misty gave Ash a sympathetic look. "Chill out, Ash. Why are you acting so tough?"

"I don't have to act tough," Ash informed her sternly. "I am tough, and so is Charizard, and we have the power to prove it!"

"Chaaaar!" Ash's Charizard agreed. It reared back its head and breathed a huge stream of fire.

Liza frowned. "Only weak Pokémon show off like that," she told Ash. "Your Charizard could use some serious training."

Ash had heard enough. "Comments like that burn me up!" he shouted.

"Chaaaar!" Ash's Pokémon let loose with another stream of fire. Ash had to duck to avoid getting fried. But he didn't duck far enough. The next thing he knew, the seat of his jeans was in flames!

Luckily, there was a huge lake in the Charicific Valley. Unluckily, it was at the bottom of a long, steep flight of stairs. Ash yelled as he ran all the way down. With one last shout, he dove into the lake.

Of course, the water was freezing. Ash groaned. So far, he hated everything about the Charicific Valley!

3

Ash's Charizard vs. the Wild Charizard

"See, didn't I tell you not to play with fire?" Liza asked.

Ash was dripping wet and humiliated. But he felt Liza was being unfair. His Charizard was great. He'd have to make her understand.

"My Charizard made it here, didn't it?" he told Liza.

Liza shrugged. "Any old Charizard should be able to reach this valley," she said. "But the Charizard in this valley aren't just any old Charizard."

"Are you saying that my Charizard is weaker than all the Charizard here?" Ash asked in disbelief. "'Cause you're way wrong!"

Liza shook her head. "The Charizard in this valley are very high level. You don't have a chance against them, but if you want to try . . ."

"We'll give it a shot," Ash replied. "Go, Charizard! You against that one!"

Ash pointed at Liza's Charizard. His own Charizard roared. Charla jerked its head back in surprise.

"Hold on," Liza said quickly. "Not against my Charla. It's not a wild Charizard — it's my pet."

"Okay, fine," Ash answered. "We'll battle anyone.

Bring 'em on!"

"*Char.*" Ash could see that his Pokémon was eager to battle.

"Okay," Liza agreed, "I'll open the gate." She aimed a remote-control device at a solid iron gate that was built into the mountain side.

Ash gasped. Behind the gate were dozens of Charizard. Some flew. Some wrestled each other. Some just lazed in the sun. All of them looked extremely big and strong.

"Those Charizard are huge!" Ash pointed out.

Liza nodded. "They're bigger than normal Charizard."

She pointed out an especially large Pokémon. "Do you think you can beat that Charizard?"

"It's gigantic!" Ash exclaimed.

"A Charizard's skill is not a matter of body size," Liza corrected him. "That Charizard is the gentlest of any in this valley."

Ash looked at his Charizard. "What do you want to do?"

"*Char!*" Charizard was eager to face an opponent. It turned to the huge Charizard and breathed a stream of fire.

Ash clenched his fists nervously. He was afraid to see what the wild Charizard would do. To his surprise, it just stood there.

"Did that do it?" Ash asked.

The big Charizard turned away from his.

"Ha! It's running away!" Ash exclaimed.

Liza shook her head. "Don't count on it!"

Suddenly, orange-and-yellow flames filled the air. The wild Charizard was swinging its flaming tail.

"Charizard!" Ash screamed. The wild Charizard lashed out at Ash's Charizard. The powerful tail of the wild Charizard smacked Charizard across the neck. The smack sent Ash's Charizard flying backward.

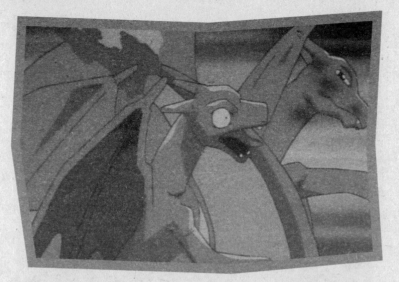

Charizard flapped its wings frantically, but it was no use. The Pokémon fell forward onto its face.

Ash ran to its side. "Hang in there, Charizard!"

"It just doesn't have the power to match the Charicific Valley Charizard yet," Liza insisted.

Ash knew she was right. But his Charizard wasn't ready to admit it. His Pokémon got to its feet. It threw back its head and breathed fire into the sky.

"Settle down, Charizard," Ash begged. "You'll always be the best Pokémon for me. We've still got lots more battles to face together."

But Charizard wasn't about to give up. It stomped toward its opponent.

Liza shrugged. "If it doesn't give up now, I won't be responsible for what happens."

"That's enough, Charizard!" Ash said.

But Charizard just kept going. *Charizard isn't making me look like much of a Trainer,* Ash thought.

His Charizard stormed up to the wild Charizard. It gave the other Charizard its toughest look.

The wild Charizard wasn't fooled for a second. With one swipe of its tail, it sent Ash's Charizard flying.

Blam! Ash's Charizard smashed into the mountain side. "Charizard!" Ash screamed.

Misty stared at the wild Charizard. "That's the gentlest one?" she asked.

"It's pretty brutal!" Brock exclaimed.

"Charizard!" Ash yelled. He couldn't believe it. Once again, Charizard had gotten to its feet. And it was heading straight for the wild Charizard.

This time, the wild Charizard had had enough. It picked up its challenger and lifted the smaller Pokémon over its head. Then it threw Ash's Charizard as hard as it could.

Charizard went flying through the air. It sailed all the way through the gate and landed at the bottom of the long staircase.

Ash, Misty, and Brock ran to the top of the stairs. Ash was afraid that his Pokémon might really be hurt this time. To his amazement, Charizard was already climbing the steep staircase. Ash could tell by the look on its face that it still wanted to battle.

Liza watched from the other side of the gate. "Sorry. You just don't have what it takes to battle the Charizard here. Go on home," she said.

Charizard kept marching. Finally, Liza aimed the remote and shut the gate tightly.

Charizard still wouldn't stop. Furious, it began pounding on the gate with its fists.

The doors of the gate slid open again. Liza stood there, looking disgusted. "You leave me no choice," she told Charizard.

"Charizard!" The stubborn Pokémon was anxious to battle.

"If you must battle someone . . ." Liza went on. She glanced over her shoulder at her pet Charizard. "My Charla has never been much for battles, but here goes."

Charla let out a little roar. *It's just a pet,* Ash thought. *Maybe Charizard has a chance.*

Wrong again! It took Charla only a second to grab Charizard and hurl it through the gate.

Charizard sailed back down the stairs. It landed in the lake with a tremendous splash.

"Hey, that's . . ." Ash began, running toward Charizard.

". . . cruel," Misty finished.

"Charizard hates water!" Brock added.

Liza gave Ash a stern look. "Your Charizard will be fine as long as its flame doesn't go out," she said coldly. Then she turned to Charizard.

"Sit there. Cool down. And think about how you can improve yourself." Liza turned away, strode through the gate, and shut it behind her.

From a nearby mountain peak, Team Rocket watched through binoculars.

Meowth, a white Pokémon with whiskers, pointed ears, and a curly tail, wiped a tear from its eye. "That Charizard fought with all its might! I hate to see it give up."

James, a boy with blue hair, nodded. "You know, Charizard kind of reminds me of us. We fight as hard as we can, too, but we always lose."

Jessie, a girl with long red hair, frowned. "We wouldn't lose if you two weren't always messing up my brilliant schemes," she said. "But I agree. Seeing Charizard like this just breaks my heart."

"You have a heart?" James asked.

Jessie smacked him on the head. "I know we came here to steal Pikachu. But I think it's time for a change of plans. We losers have to stick together."

Meowth nodded. "Let Operation Save Charizard Begin!"

Good-Bye, Charizard

"I can't believe Charizard won't get out of the lake," Misty said. She clutched her Togepi. It was dark now and getting cold.

Ash was worried, too. Charizard's tail stuck out of the water. The flame on the tip still burned, but not as brightly as before.

Ash walked to the edge of the lake. "Enough, Charizard. Give it up," he said.

Charizard shook its head.

"Do you really hate losing that much?" Ash asked.

Charizard nodded sadly.

Ash wished he could talk Charizard into leaving the

lake. But Charizard was too stubborn! *A really good Trainer would know what to do,* he told himself. But Ash couldn't think of anything.

After a while, he felt too tired to think at all. Feeling sad, he joined Brock and Misty, who were sleeping on the steps.

Several hours later, the sun rose over the Charicific Valley. Ash woke up and ran to the edge of the lake. Charizard's flame still burned. But the Pokémon looked even sadder than before.

"Charizard, I know you don't feel strong enough. But you're good enough for me," Ash began. Suddenly, his speech was interrupted by a loud noise.

"Hey, what's that?" Ash asked. He turned and

discovered a very strange sight. A mechanical man stomped toward the gate that protected the wild Charizard. The robot was as tall as a house. It wore a safari hat and carried a large net. On its shirtfront was a logo Ash had seen many times.

"Team Rocket!" Ash yelled. "What do you think you're doing?"

"We don't have time to answer," Meowth replied, from inside the mechanical man.

Ash could hear Jessie, too. "This is the only way to get Charizard out," she said.

Team Rocket steered the robot into the gate. The mechanical man pounded on the heavy doors.

"Chaaar!" roared the Fire-type Pokémon. Charizard climbed out of the lake. It was not about to let Team Rocket steal any wild Charizard.

Charizard hurried up the steps. It shoved itself between the robot and the gate.

"It's right in front of us," Jessie said.

"Just like we planned," James added.

"It's trying to protect the wild Charizard," Jessie went on.

What are they thinking? Ash wondered. They almost seemed to be trying to get Charizard to attack them!

Of course, that was exactly what Charizard did. *"Charizard!"* The big Pokémon threw back its head. It breathed a huge stream of fire all over the mechanical man. The robot just stood there. Team Rocket didn't even try to get out of Charizard's way!

"Just like we predicted!" Jessie shouted.

"That's right!" Meowth agreed.

Suddenly, it dawned on Ash. Team Rocket had made Charizard get out of the lake! Now it looked like they were trying to build its confidence by letting it win. Ash wasn't sure why the villains were trying to help Charizard, but he didn't care.

Charizard kept on blasting the robot. Smoke began pouring from its metal safari hat. But still, Team Rocket didn't move.

Suddenly, the safari hat blew off. A second later, the entire mechanical man exploded! Jessie, James, and Meowth flew out. As they soared into the sky, they called out to Charizard.

"You're very brave, Charizard," James shouted.

"You can get stronger," Meowth said.

"But as for Team Rocket . . ." Jessie cried.

"We're blasting off again!" the whole team shouted.

Ash ran to Charizard. "You did it!"

"Pika!" Ash could tell that Pikachu was proud of Charizard, too. The Pokémon was a winner again.

The gate to the Charizard area slid open. Liza and Charla stood there. Liza clapped. Charla looked pleased, too.

Liza looked at Charizard. "You can join us now, if you want," Liza said.

Ash understood what Liza meant. She was inviting Charizard to stay and train in the Charicific Valley.

"Why now?" Ash asked. "I thought Charizard couldn't cut it here."

"Because your Charizard is so determined," Liza answered. "And I think it learned something from its night in the lake. It's ready to learn from its own kind now."

The Fire-type Pokémon gathered behind Liza. They looked at Ash's Charizard expectantly.

This was all happening so fast. Ash knew training in the valley would be good for his Charizard. But how could he let it go? He and Charizard had been through so much together. He'd never forget the first time he met that cute little Charmander. Or when Charmander evolved into Charmeleon. They were some of the best moments of his life.

And now Charizard was one of his strongest Pokémon. Ash would miss Charizard, but he'd also have a hard time winning battles without it.

Ash took a deep breath. This wasn't his decision to make. He turned to Charizard.

"What do you want to do?" Ash asked.

Charizard turned and stared at him. Ash could tell by the look on its face that it wanted to stay in the valley. But it didn't want to hurt Ash's feelings.

That look told Ash all he needed to know. He stared at the ground. "Well, I guess this is good-bye," he said. "You've got a lot to learn, Charizard, and you'd better get started."

He pulled his baseball cap down low. He couldn't let

Charizard see how sad he felt.

"Get out of here!" Ash told it firmly. He pointed to the wild Charizard. In a gentler voice he said, "You're not meant to follow me, Charizard. You belong with them."

"*Charizard!*" The Pokémon gave Ash one last, long look. Then it turned to join the other Charizard.

Ash began to run. He had to get out of that valley before he changed his mind. "Train hard," he called to Charizard. "We'll meet again – when you're the strongest Pokémon in the world!"

Ash kept on running and didn't look back. He knew he was doing the right thing. But saying good-bye to Charizard was one of the most painful things he'd ever had to do.

5

GligarMan to the Rescue!

"What was that noise?" Misty asked.

"I'd say a Pidgeot or maybe a Hoothoot," Ash replied.

"It sounded different to me," Brock put in.

A few days had passed. Ash and his friends were hiking through a forest. As usual, Pikachu was riding on Ash's baseball cap, and Misty was holding Togepi in her arms.

Ash was still feeling sad about Charizard. Even the thought of getting another badge didn't thrill him like it used to. Besides, he wasn't even sure if he could win without Charizard.

But right now, Ash had a minor Pokémon mystery on his hands. An unidentified Flying-type Pokémon had just called out from the treetops.

Suddenly, the Pokémon flew right over their heads. It was purple and had wings, and the curved claws of an insect. It also had a long tail with a sharp point on the end.

"Did you see that?" Ash shouted.

"Was it really a Pokémon?" Misty asked.

"I'm pretty sure it was a Gligar!" Brock told them.

Quickly, Ash dug into his pocket and pulled out Dexter, his Pokédex. The tiny computer held information about all the world's Pokémon.

"Gligar, the Fly Scorpio Pokémon, uses the capelike wings on its back to travel easily from tree to tree," Dexter recited.

"It looks kind of spooky," Misty said.

"It doesn't get along well with humans," Brock informed them.

"Well, I think it's cool," Ash said. He was always happy to see a new type of Pokémon. "Come on out again, Gligar. Come out, wherever you are!"

Ash, Misty, and Brock looked at the sky, hoping to spot the Gligar again. Suddenly, Ash felt the ground give way underneath them.

Ash landed with a thud inside a hole in the ground. Misty, Brock, and Pikachu landed beside him. Everyone seemed to be okay. But what was going on?

Ash looked up to see Jessie, James, and Meowth looming over the hole.

Ash groaned. He should have known. Team Rocket

had been a big help with Charizard. But now they were
back to their usual tricks!

Jessie cackled. "Prepare for trouble!" she chanted.

"And make it double!" James added.

"Cut it out!" Ash moaned. He'd had enough of Team
Rocket.

But Team Rocket was feeling smug. "We've hit a
peak already!" Meowth shouted. "Our pitfall plan is a
success!"

Jessie and James wheeled a strange device to the
edge of the hole. It looked sort of like a fire hydrant,
with two levers and a hose attached to it.

Jessie and James began pumping the levers. Meowth
grabbed the hose and aimed it at the hole. In seconds,

Ash and his friends were standing in water up to their knees.

I'll show them, Ash thought. "Go, Pikachu!"

"Pika!" The little Electric-type Pokémon stood on Ash's head and prepared to launch its Thundershock attack.

"Wait a minute!" Misty shouted. Just in time, she and Brock grabbed Pikachu and stopped it.

"Water conducts electricity," Brock explained. "If Pikachu attacks now, we'll be electrocuted."

What do I do now? Ash wondered. He wished he had his Charizard. It might not be the strongest Pokémon in the world. But it was strong enough to deal with Team Rocket.

"If you want out, just hand over Pikachu," Jessie cackled. She and James began pumping harder. Suddenly, a jet of water blasted Togepi out of Misty's arms. The little Pokémon could not swim.

"Togepi!" Misty screamed.

"Togi, togi," it cried, struggling to stay afloat.

"Gligar!" Out of nowhere, the mysterious Pokémon swooped to Togepi's rescue. It snatched the small Pokémon and carried it safely to a tree branch.

Then a very strange man climbed onto the branch

beside Gligar. He was dressed from head to toe in a crazy purple costume with tights, boots, a big purple cape, and a mask that covered his eyes and nose. On his hands, he wore gloves that looked like Gligar's claws.

The masked man pointed at Team Rocket. "Stop right there, evildoers!" he commanded. Team Rocket stared at him. They looked as shocked as Ash felt.

The man began to chant. "When voices cry out for aid, the ears of GligarMan hear them. When evildoers do evil stuff, the eyes of GligarMan see them. And then the claws of GligarMan stop them!"

The man raised his arms above his head and stood on one foot. His Gligar did the same. They looked kind of cool, for a second. Then the guy slipped and had to hug the branch to keep from falling out of the tree.

"Who is this guy?" Ash asked.

"I've never heard of him," Brock replied.

"What a weird old guy," Meowth said.

"I'm no old guy. I'm a superhero!" GligarMan protested.

"A superhero, huh?" Jessie sneered. "You don't look like one to me."

"I said I'm a superhero and I mean it!" the purple guy insisted. He raised his fists in the air and bounced up and down on one leg.

"*Gligar!*" Gligar copied the man's actions.

GligarMan must be okay, Ash thought, *because that Gligar sure admires him.*

"He may be for real," Misty said. "After all, he saved Togepi."

GligarMan smiled. "Thank you for your faith, unnamed girl."

"My name is Misty," Misty told him.

"Pleased to meet you, Miss Misty," said GligarMan. "Never fear, your rescue is at hand! Go, Gligar! Banish those evildoers!"

"Gligar!" Gligar sailed out of the tree. It landed on Jessie's face and hung on tight!

Jessie let out a bloodcurdling scream. "My face! What are you doing? I can't see anything."

James and Meowth ran around Jessie in crazy circles. Ash supposed that they were trying to help her, but as usual, they were useless.

"Get it off! Get it off!" Jessie shrieked at them. "Get this thing off my face!"

"Okay, okay, settle down," James told her. "I'll have

it off in a second." Cautiously, he reached for the tip of Gligar's tail.

GligarMan chuckled. "Never underestimate the power of Gligar's tail needle!" he shouted.

Immediately, James pulled his hand away. "Go, Meowth!" he commanded.

"Fury swipes!" the Scratch Cat Pokémon screamed. It threw itself at Jessie and Gligar. It slashed at Gligar with its claws.

Gligar let go and flew away. Meowth was still swiping. Its claws made a big scratch on Jessie's face.

Jessie was furious. She lashed out at Meowth. Soon, the two were racing around in circles, attacking each other. Then Gligar flew back again, aiming right

for Jessie's head.

Jessie couldn't take it anymore. She turned and ran, with James and Meowth right behind her.

"Good work, Gligar," GligarMan said. "Strike the victory pose." As before, Trainer and Pokémon raised their arms and stood on one foot.

"Thanks for saving Togepi, Mr. GligarMan," Misty said.

"I'll bring this Togepi back to you right now," GligarMan said. He grabbed Togepi and leaped off the tree branch. "Gligar, jump!" he yelled.

Apparently, GligarMan had forgotten that he could not fly. "I'm falling! Help me, Gligar!" The superhero crash-landed in a bush. But he managed to keep Togepi from getting hurt.

"Thanks again!" Misty said, grabbing the Spike Ball Pokémon.

GligarMan crawled back into the bushes and came back riding a motorcycle. He handed Ash and his friends a whistle. The whistle had a Gligar logo on it.

"I shall always be watching over you," he said solemnly. "Should you require the aid of GligarMan again, just blow this whistle." Then he called for his Gligar and rode away.

Seconds later, a teenage girl came along on a bike. She was riding really fast and she looked kind of upset. When she saw Ash and his friends, she skidded to a stop. "Did you just see GligarMan here?" she asked.

"Uh, yeah," Misty answered her.

"I hope he didn't cause you any trouble," the girl said.

"Not at all. In fact, he saved my Togepi," Misty assured her.

"That's a relief!" the girl sighed.

As usual, Brock had an instant crush on the girl.

"My name is Brock and yours is . . . ?"

"My name is Latoya," the girl told him.

"Just who is GligarMan, anyway, Latoya?" Ash asked. "Is he really a superhero?"

Latoya shrugged. She looked embarrassed. "He thinks he is, but sometimes he goes too far and causes more harm than good."

Ash could see how that might be true. Still, GligarMan had saved him and his friends. And he was definitely an awesome Gligar Trainer.

"Do you know his true identity?" Ash asked.

The question seemed to make Latoya nervous. "No, no!" she shouted. "I'm just glad he didn't bother you." She popped a wheelie and rode away.

"I'd sure like to meet them again," Ash said.

Brock's eyes lit up. "Me, too. I want to see Latoya again."

"I was talking about GligarMan," Ash yelled. "To handle a Gligar that well, he must be a great Trainer!"

"Come on," Brock said. "Let's go find Latoya and GligarMan!"

The Secret
of GligarMan

Ash and his friends didn't walk far before they came to a town. The first building they saw had a tall tower with a purple, Gligar-shaped logo on it.

Brock pulled out the Gligar whistle. "Look, it's got the same logo as that building!"

Ash peeked though the door. Inside the big building, there was a little toy store jam-packed with Gligar and GligarMan merchandise.

"Wow, GligarMan must be really popular here," Misty said.

"Come on inside," called a voice from the store. "Step right up!"

"Hey, that was Latoya's voice!" Brock pushed Ash aside and ran into the store.

Ash and Misty quickly followed. Sure enough, there was Latoya, standing behind the sales counter.

"Hey, it's you guys again!" she exclaimed.

"You've got to tell me more about GligarMan," Ash begged her.

A door near the sales counter opened. A tall man in a cowboy hat walked into the room. "I can you tell all about GligarMan," he announced.

"Dad!" Latoya said.

"I am the store owner," the man explained. "I know more about GligarMan than anyone in town."

"Really?" Ash was very excited.

"GligarMan has been fighting crime in this town for years," the man said. "He mesmerizes criminals with his massive muscles and his amazing moves."

"Are you sure we're talking about the same Gligar-Man?" Ash asked. "I mean, he was pretty cool, but I don't remember any massive muscles."

"The GligarMan we saw had some moves all

right," added Brock. "But I wouldn't exactly call them amazing."

Latoya's dad blushed. "No, no, GligarMan really is amazing!" he said. "He's big and tough and strong."

"I don't care if GligarMan has muscles or not," Misty said. "He and Gligar saved Togepi. That proves he's a hero to me."

"Togi, togi, togepi!" Togepi jumped down from Misty's arms. It hopped up and down and tugged at the store owner's pant leg.

Misty thought she knew why. "You're the real Gligar-Man, aren't you, sir?"

Latoya's dad snorted. "What are you talking about, Misty? Of course I'm not GligarMan."

"Really?" Misty asked. "The only person in this town who knows my name is GligarMan!"

Latoya's dad gritted his teeth. "I blew it," he admitted.

Ash was excited. "GligarMan, I have to know. How did you learn to handle your Gligar so well?" he asked

GligarMan put a finger to his lips. "Shhhh! You can't let my true identity get out."

GligarMan led everyone through a side door. Latoya came along, too. They got into an elevator and rode to the top of Gligar Tower. All the while, GligarMan talked about GligarMan.

"Papa, I'm sure these kids have heard enough about your hobbies," Latoya scolded.

"It's no hobby! Being GligarMan is my destiny,"

GligarMan insisted. "To stop the spread of evil and fill the world with truth and love, that is the noble goal of GligarMan!"

"I wish he'd give it up," Latoya said. "He's getting too old for this stuff."

"GligarMan will never give up!" GligarMan declared. "Not as long as there are people who need me."

"I still think you need help," Latoya grumbled.

Ash understood. GligarMan was really cool. But as superheroes went, he wasn't perfect.

The elevator stopped at the top of Gligar Tower. The doors slid open. "We've arrived at my secret base, everyone," said GligarMan.

Ash and his friends gasped. "Wow! This place is awesome!" Ash said.

The secret base was a huge, dark room with very high ceilings. It was filled with video screens and interesting-looking control panels. Gligar was in there, sitting on a structure that looked like a huge jungle gym.

"*Gligar.*" The Pokémon leaped from the jungle gym. It landed happily in its Trainer's arms.

"You must be serious about your mission, to have

built a room like this," Misty said to GligarMan.

"It's great that you're working this hard against evil," Ash added. "I really look up to you, GligarMan."

It was true. GligarMan was not just a talented Pokémon Trainer. He was putting his talent to good use, helping people and fighting evil. Ash admired him very much.

Suddenly, a high-pitched whistle sounded in the Gligar base room.

"Huh?" Ash asked.

"That's the Gligar whistle," GligarMan shouted. "Someone is calling for help!" He ran to a control panel and flipped some switches. A row of video screens lit up.

Ash gasped when he saw what was on the screens. Criminals had invaded the toy shop.

"My store is under attack. Gligar, it's time to move!"

In a flash, GligarMan had changed into his crime-fighting costume. He and Gligar were ready to go.

Ash turned to Pikachu. "Let's go, too!"

Attack of the
Metapod Man

"Stop right there, evildoers!" GligarMan commanded.

Ash, GligarMan, and their Pokémon stood in the doorway of the toy shop. Inside the store was an ugly scene. Toys and costumes had been tossed all over the floor. Two of the villains were wearing yellow-green costumes. They looked like Metapod, a Cocoon Pokémon that evolve from Caterpie.

A red-haired girl in a black leather outfit seemed to be running the show. Ash recognized her instantly.

"Jessie from Team Rocket!" he yelled. "I should have known it was you."

Jessie threw back her head and laughed. "So you've finally made it. GligarMan and the twerp. Last time, we had our guard down, but this time we're ready."

Jessie leaped high in the air. "Go, Metapod Man!" she shouted.

"Right!" said Meowth, from inside a Metapod suit. "We'll see if these phony villain costumes work."

James also wore a Metapod suit. He leaped up to attack first.

"Go Gligar!" shouted GligarMan.

"Gligar!" The Pokémon flew at the fake Metapod. It latched onto James's head with its claws.

"Help me, help me!" James screamed.

"Time for stage two, Meowth," Jessie said.

Meowth scurried behind the sales counter. When it returned, it was riding inside a huge mechanical bug. It looked like a Spinarak, a Pokémon Ash had seen before on his journey. This Bug- and Poison-type Pokémon was made of green plastic, with yellow plastic legs and big red fangs. A black tube protruded beneath its mouth.

"Go, Mecha-Spinarak!" shouted Meowth. Mecha-Spinarak marched toward Ash, Pikachu, and GligarMan.

"Hey! Cut it out! Stop!" Ash and GligarMan yelled.

"Pika!" Pikachu agreed.

Inside the Spinarak, Meowth pressed a button. Sticky

53

white thread shot out of the tube from the Spinarak's mouth. It slapped against Ash and stuck to him. "Hey, let go of me!" Ash shouted.

But the sticky thread kept on coming. It wound around and around Ash, Pikachu, and GligarMan. Suddenly, Ash realized what was happening. Meowth was wrapping them in a cocoon!

In seconds, Ash, Pikachu, and GligarMan were wrapped so tightly they could barely move at all. Jessie cackled with glee. "Now it's all over for you!"

Meowth pulled a lever. The Mecha-Spinarak smashed through a wall of the store, dragging Ash and the others with it.

Outside, Meowth made the mechanical Bug-type Pokémon stand up on its back pair of legs. It whipped the big cocoon through the air and left it hanging from a street lamp!

Jessie and James walked through the hole in the wall. Gligar still clung to James's head. "Looks like the bad guys win," Jessie laughed.

"No way!" Ash protested. "This is not over yet!" He, Pikachu, and GligarMan struggled to get free.

"Struggle all you like," Jessie cackled. "It won't get you anywhere."

Ash looked down. Misty and Brock were on the ground, along with a whole bunch of people from the town. But none of them could do anything to help.

"GligarMan!" Ash hoped the superhero would have an idea. But GligarMan just groaned.

"You can do it, GligarMan," a voice called out. The whole crowd looked to see where it was coming from. A girl stood on the top of Gligar Tower. She wore a uniform very much like GligarMan's.

"Who are you, anyway?" Jessie shouted.

"I am . . . Gligirl!"

"Gligirl, take care of Team Rocket," Misty pleaded.

Gligirl pointed at the giant cocoon. "Gligar, cut the thread that's tying them up!" she commanded.

The purple Pokémon let go of James's head and flew at

the cocoon. It slashed through the thread with its claws. Ash, Pikachu, and GligarMan tumbled to the ground.

Ask leaped to his feet. "All right! It's our turn to attack. Go, Pikachu!"

"*Pika!*" Pikachu raced at the Mecha-Spinarak. It darted in and out among the Bug-type Pokémon's legs.

Meowth worked the controls, trying to crush Pikachu with the legs. Instead, all six legs collapsed. Mecha-Spinarak crashed to the ground in a heap.

Lightning-quick Pikachu escaped unharmed. "*Pika, pika,*" it said gleefully.

Jessie was furious. "Catch it, James!" she shrieked.

James lunged at Pikachu. At the same time, Gligirl leaped down from the tower and landed beside Ash. "Gligar, Poison Sting attack," she shouted.

Gligar aimed its tail needle at James and fired a series of darts.

"Help me!" James began racing back and forth, trying to escape the attack.

It's time to finish this off! Ash thought. "Pikachu, Thunderbolt!"

"*Pika!*" The little Pokémon nailed Mecha-Spinarak with a mighty jolt of electricity.

Meowth had had enough. It jammed a lever inside the Mecha-Spinarak and began chasing James and Jessie out of town.

"Okay, enough, don't come any closer!" screamed Jessie and James.

Too late. The effects of Pikachu's Thunderbolt attack combined with the running, caused the Mecha-Spinarak to explode! The force propelled Jessie, James, and Meowth into the sky.

"Looks like Team Rocket's blasting off again!" they shouted.

"We did it!" Ash cheered.

"Gligirl is born," GligarMan said proudly.

"But where did Latoya go?" Brock wondered.

Gligirl took off her mask and revealed her true identity. She was Latoya, of course.

"What made you want to become Gligirl?" Ash asked.

"When I saw my father tied up, I had to do something," Latoya answered. "The next thing I knew, I was wearing that costume."

"We're all Gligar in this family," GligarMan beamed.

"And if I become Gligirl, Papa can finally retire," Latoya said.

"Maybe someday," GligarMan said. "But I'm not giving up yet."

Ash grinned. GligarMan was kind of nutty, but he was a true superhero. Ash hoped he'd find a way to help others as much as GligarMan did.

The sun was setting as Ash and his friends prepared to leave town.

"Say, Ash," GligarMan said. "Don't forget your Gligar whistle. Blow it anytime, and I'll be there."

"Okay, thanks," Ash agreed.

"Hey, Latoya," Brock asked. "What should I do to call Gligirl?"

"You won't need to," Misty sighed. "Come on, let's go."

And so Ash and his friends said good-bye to the Gligar family, and set off in search of Johto League Gyms.

8

The Search for Cyndaquil

"So, Ash," Misty said as they headed to the next town, "do you still miss Charizard?"

"I'll always miss Charizard," Ash said. "But I have to admit that GligarMan cheered me up a little. That guy never gives up. And I won't give up, either. I'll prove I can win gym badges even without Charizard."

"We have to get to a gym first," Brock said. He studied a map. "I can't figure out where we are."

Ash, Misty, and Brock were trying to find a place called Azalea Town. But, as usual, they had gotten lost in the middle of a dense forest.

Ash had no patience for maps. He just wanted to keep moving. "Let's cut straight through the forest. Maybe we'll find our way back to the main road."

Misty didn't look too thrilled by that suggestion. But before an argument could start, the friends were interrupted by a shout.

"Hey, you guys!" A Pokémon Trainer came striding through the trees. He had long brown hair and wore blue jeans, a black shirt, and a red vest.

"Have you seen any Cyndaquil around here?" he asked.

Cyndaquil?! Ash had wanted to catch a Cyndaquil ever since he first saw one in New Bark Town. "Did you say Cyndaquil?" he asked. "Where are they?"

The kid scowled. "Like I know? I just heard that there were some around here."

Ash was already pawing through some bushes. "Come on out, Cyndaquil."

The boy's eyes flashed angrily. "Hey! Listen, kid. You'd better stay away from the Cyndaquil here. They belong to me!"

Ash ignored him. He knew that wild Pokémon did not belong to anyone – until they were caught fair and square.

"Cyndaquil!" Ash called.

"Hey, punk, are you listening to me?" the boy was really angry now.

But Ash wasn't paying attention. He hurried down a path through the forest.

"Cyndaquil, Cyndaquil, come on, Cyndaquil!" Ash called. But no Cyndaquil appeared. "Pikachu, help me find a Cyndaquil."

"*Pika, pika!*" The little yellow Pokémon hopped down from Ash's shoulder and scurried along the path.

"Can you sense a Cyndaquil anywhere, Pikachu?" Ash asked it.

"*Pika.*" The little Pokémon shook its head sadly.

"Keep looking." Ash was sure they'd spot a Cyndaquil sooner or later.

"Wait right there, twerp!" a mechanical voice boomed.

Ash looked up. A giant robot loomed on the path in front of them.

Ash's mouth fell open. The robot was taller than the trees. It looked like an enormous Meowth.

A trapdoor opened in the robot's head. Jessie, James, and Meowth came riding through the door on a elevator platform.

"Hand over that Pikachu!" Meowth demanded.

"I'm in a hurry," Ash told them. "So get out of my way. Pikachu, Thunderbolt!"

"Pikaaaa!" The Electric-type Pokémon blasted Robot Meowth with a huge bolt of lightning.

Team Rocket howled with laughter. "All of that energy just goes to power this robot," Meowth screeched.

"Fire the cat's-paw bubble-gum launchers," James ordered.

The robot's arms swung up from its sides. Enormous wads of pink bubble gum shot out of the paws.

Gross! Ash thought. The gum was soft and sticky. He and Pikachu had to duck and dodge like mad to avoid getting hit.

"This way, Pikachu!" Ash led his Pokémon through the legs of the robot. They puffed and panted as they sped away.

Ash heard a loud crash. Cool! Team Rocket had tried to make the robot do a back flip – but it had fallen flat on its back instead.

So much for their latest machine, Ash thought. He and Pikachu jogged into a clearing.

"Hey, Pikachu, look at all the caves!" Across the clearing there was a tall rock face. Several caves were dug into the rocks.

"Pikachu!" The little Pokémon sat on Ash's head.

"What, Pikachu? What do you see?" Then Ash saw it, too. High up on the side of a rock face, a small Pokémon sat on a ledge in front of a cave. The Pokémon had a beige underbelly and a blue back with red spots on it. Ash reached for his Pokédex.

"I finally found a Cyndaquil!"

9

Rescue in the Caves

"Cyndaquil, a Fire-type Pokémon, is mild-tempered," said Dexter. "But it can emit flames from its back when upset."

Ash flipped Dexter shut. "Don't move from that spot," he begged the Cyndaquil.

With Pikachu on his back, Ash scaled the rocks up to the Cyndaquil. They were almost there when a Sand-slash – a golden-brown Pokémon with quills – showed up on the ledge above them. The Sandslash dug at the ground with its claws, sending a shower of sand down the rock face.

That's a Sand attack, Ash realized. His hands and

feet slipped on the sand and he slid all the way back to the ground.

The boy they had met earlier walked up beside the Sandslash, laughing meanly. "See ya, kid," he called to Ash.

"That's not fair," Ash complained.

The boy sneered. "I got here first. That's what matters. It doesn't matter how I did it."

"Cynda." The Cyndaquil did not look eager for the boy to catch it. It shook its head nervously and scampered into the cave.

The boy and Sandslash were right behind it. "Sandslash, catch that Cyndaquil," Ash heard the boy say.

"Pika!" Pikachu said, sounding worried.

"You're right, Pikachu," Ash agreed. "I can't lose to a loser like that!"

Quickly, Ash scrambled back up the rocks. As he crawled onto the ledge, he heard voices behind him. Team Rocket had arrived again in their Robot Meowth.

"We won't let you get away this time," Jessie screeched.

Ash turned and waved them off. "Sorry, but I don't have time for you now." He and Pikachu turned again and ran into the cave.

"Wow! It's like a maze in here." The cave was a bunch of rooms, connected by tunnels. Ash saw the Cyndaquil right away.

"Cynda," it called to him. It sounded happy that he had found it. Unfortunately, the boy and Sandslash heard it, too. As they raced into the room, Sandslash knocked Ash off his feet.

"Oof!" By the time Ash picked himself up, Cyndaquil had run away, with the boy in hot pursuit.

Ash hurried after them. Soon, he was in a big room with several tunnels leading out of it. The boy and the Cyndaquil were nowhere to be seen. And Ash had no idea which way to go.

"Pika, pikachu!" the Pokémon cried in alarm. An enormous gumball came bouncing through the tunnel. Team Rocket had found them. The giant gumball headed straight for Ash and Pikachu.

"Yikes!" There was no time to decide which way to go. Ash and Pikachu raced into the nearest tunnel to avoid getting crushed.

They got to the next room just in time. The boy, Sandslash, and Cyndaquil were in there.

The boy barked an order to his Pokémon. "Sandslash, use Poison Sting!"

What a rotten way to catch a new Pokémon! Ash thought. He scooped up Cyndaquil and kept on running.

The gigantic gumball was still coming. Ash darted away from it, into another tunnel. He was pleased to hear the boy get knocked down by the ball.

Ash ran and ran as the ball bounced closer and closer. Finally, he saw a light. The end of the tunnel came not a moment too soon. With a loud *ka-boom*, the gumball exploded. Ash clutched Pikachu and Cyndaquil and dove for the mouth of the tunnel.

They landed hard and skidded across the rocky ground. *We're back in the clearing*, Ash realized. "Pikachu, Cyndaquil, are you all right?"

"*Pika!*"

"*Cynda!*"

Both Pokémon seemed as good as ever. Ash figured his problems were finally over. Then he looked up. Oops! He was standing at the feet of Robot Meowth.

"Cat's-paw bubble-gum machine, fire one round!" James ordered.

Ash tried to dodge the flying wads of gum. But he had nowhere to go. He was trapped between the robot and the rock. *Ka-blam!* Team Rocket scored a direct hit. The gum missed Cyndaquil by inches. But Ash and Pikachu were trapped in the gooey mess!

Cyndaquil vs. Sandslash

"We did it!" Team Rocket cheered.

Then Meowth noticed the little Fire-type Pokémon. "Hey, it's a Cyndaquil," Meowth said.

"Why don't we catch it, too?" James suggested.

Ash turned to the Pokémon. "Run, Cyndaquil! You can get away," he told it.

Cyndaquil hesitated. Ash realized it did not want to leave them.

"We'll be fine," Ash promised. "You run for it. Hurry!"

At last, Cyndaquil began scampering across the rocks.

"Not so fast," James's voice boomed out.

"I'll give it a punch to weaken it," Meowth cackled. *Ker-pow!* Robot Meowth's arm shot forward. Its paw missed Cyndaquil and blasted a hole in the rock.

"Run away, Cyndaquil," Ash told it.

But Cyndaquil didn't move. It stared at the robot. Suddenly, it threw its head back and gave a mighty roar. *"Cyyynndaaaquiiillll!"*

Ash gasped. Flames were shooting out of Cyndaquil's

back! All at once, the Pokémon's flames became an inferno. A ball of fire engulfed Robot Meowth.

"Wow!" Ash yelled. Cyndaquil's Flamethrower attack was almost as powerful as Charizard's.

The charred robot rumbled. Sparks flew from its parts. Ash could see that it was going to explode.

"If we don't do something, Cyndaquil will get caught in the blast," he shouted. "Pikachu, Thunderbolt!"

"*Pika,*" Pikachu said. The yellow Pokémon was afraid that Ash would get hurt.

"I'll be fine. Just do it." Ash closed his eyes and braced himself.

"*Pika pi!*" Pikachu's ears stood up straight as it let loose a Thunderbolt. The force shattered the gum wad and sent the pieces flying. Ash and Pikachu were free.

But Cyndaquil was still in danger. Ash grabbed a Poké Ball and threw it hard. He knew that Cyndaquil would be safe inside it.

The Poké Ball got there in the nick of time. With a tremendous boom, the robot exploded into dust.

The blast sent Ash and Pikachu flying. Ash grabbed Pikachu and hung on tight.

Team Rocket soared into the sky. "Looks like Team

Rocket's blasting off again!" they screamed.

Ash looked up from the rock where he'd landed. The Poké Ball was lying a few yards away.

Ash checked to be sure that Pikachu was all right. Then he made a beeline for the Poké Ball.

Ash grabbed the Poké Ball and threw it. Cyndaquil appeared, blinking and shaking its head.

"Did you get hurt, Cyndaquil?"

"*Cynda,*" the Pokémon said.

"That's good," Ash said. It was fine.

Ash squatted down to question Cyndaquil. "Back there, did you use that attack to help me and Pikachu?"

"*Cyndaquil!*" The Pokémon nodded.

"Hey, Cyndaquil, you're not just powerful . . . you're really nice, too!"

"Cynda." The Pokémon looked happy.

Ash had to smile. Cyndaquil was so cute and friendly.

"Hey, Ash!" Misty's voice called out.

"Are you okay?" asked Brock.

Misty and Brock! Ash suddenly realized he hadn't seen them for a while. They must have been looking for him.

"Hey, isn't that a Cyndaquil?" Misty asked.

"Did you catch it?" Brock wondered.

"Yeah," Ash shrugged. "I was trying to help it, and I used my Poké Ball without thinking."

"Get outta my waaaayy!" The boy came roaring out of the tunnel. He was back with a vengeance.

"I'm going to catch that Cyndaquil," he shouted. "Go, Sandslash!"

"Wait!" Ash threw his hands up to stop them. "I already caught this Cyndaquil."

The boy wasn't impressed. "I'll battle you with my Sandslash, and the winner gets that Cyndaquil."

"That's ridiculous!" Brock exclaimed. "Ash already caught that Cyndaquil, so it belongs to him."

"That's right," Misty added.

"He's just afraid of losing." The boy sneered.

Ash had heard enough. He did not want to lose Cyndaquil. But he knew a Pokémon battle was the only way to get rid of the boy.

"Fine," he told the boy. "I'll take your challenge and use my Cyndaquil."

"Ash," Misty said. "You've never battled with Cyndaquil before. Are you sure you want to risk it?"

Ash nodded. "Don't worry, Misty. I've seen what Cyndaquil can do." Ash knew that its Flamethrower attack would toast Sandslash in no time.

Ash, the boy, and their Pokémon assumed battle position. "A single battle. One-on-one. Okay?" the boy asked.

"Sure. Bring it on!" Ash agreed.

The boy pumped his fist in the air. "Sandslash, Fury Swipes!"

The prickly Pokémon flew at Cyndaquil. Its razor-sharp claws were ready for action.

"Dodge it, Cyndaquil!" Ash instructed. He looked down at the Fire-type Pokémon. Huh?! Little Cyndaquil was fast asleep!

"Wake up, Cyndaquil!" Ash shouted. He gave the Pokémon a shove. It woke up just in time to roll away from the attacking Sandslash.

"Good job, Cyndaquil. Now, Flamethrower!"

Cyndaquil faced Sandslash. The Fire-type Pokémon

threw back its head and opened its mouth wide. It looked just like it did when it fried Team Rocket. But this time, no flames came out of its back.

"Cyndaquil!" Ash cried. *What was wrong with it?*

"Sandslash, finish it now with Slash!" the boy commanded.

Sandslash flew at Cyndaquil with its claws outstretched.

Quickly, Cyndaquil leaped to safety on the trunk of a nearby tree.

Sandslash was right behind it. It slashed at Cyndaquil with one razor claw. Cyndaquil dodged it just in time.

Sandslash's claw sliced right through the tree trunk! The tree crashed to the ground.

Cyndaquil jumped to another tree. Again, Sandslash swiped at it. Cyndaquil jumped away and sat panting on the ground.

"Come on, Cyndaquil," Ash encouraged it. "Pull yourself together."

"Sandslash, finish it off with your best attack," the boy ordered. "Continual Fury Swipes."

Sandslash charged at Cyndaquil. Its razor claws were ready to slash.

"Dodge them, Cyndaquil!" Ash screamed. He had seen what those claws could do to a tree. He could only imagine what they might do to Cyndaquil.

Sandslash began to swipe furiously at Cyndaquil. But Cyndaquil was too quick for Sandslash. Over and over, its claws flew at Cyndaquil with lightning speed – but Cyndaquil dodged them every time.

"Whoa, its defense is great!" Ash said proudly. "Keep it up, Cyndaquil!"

Finally, Sandslash got too tired to attack. It slumped over, puffing and panting.

"No time to rest, Sandslash," the boy yelled. "Speed Star!"

Sandslash somersaulted through the air toward Cyndaquil. It unleashed a stream of glowing white stars.

"Cyndaquil, fight back with Flamethrower," Ash instructed it. The Pokémon opened its mouth. A tiny, useless puff of smoke came out of its back.

One after another, the stars nailed Cyndaquil in the head. The little Pokémon was blasted backward. It fell on its face, dazed.

"Looks like that Cyndaquil still hasn't got its attack skills down," the boy sneered.

"You're wrong," Ash told him. Then a light dawned in Ash's mind. He crouched down beside Cyndaquil. "Does it take time for you to recover after you use an attack?" he asked.

"Cynda." The Pokémon was clearly relieved that Ash was finally getting it.

This is all my fault, Ash thought. *I shouldn't have battled with a Pokémon I hardly know anything about. I'm always getting my Pokémon in trouble.*

But there was no time to worry about that now. The boy was on the warpath. "Sandslash, use Speed Star again!"

Sandslash somersaulted toward Cyndaquil. Stars flew from its spiny body.

"Cyndaquil!" The Pokémon squealed as the stars blasted it through air. Cyndaquil hit a tree, slid down the trunk, and collapsed in a heap.

A New Member
of the Team

Ash ran to Cyndaquil's side. "Don't give up," he encouraged it. "Your speed is great. Keep dodging the attacks and you'll be fine."

The boy was already beginning to gloat. "Finish it with Fury Swipes," he shouted at Sandslash.

One more time, Sandslash charged Cyndaquil. Cyndaquil leaped straight up in the air to avoid it.

It's got an incredible vertical jump, Ash thought.

Sandslash's claw pierced the tree trunk and stuck there. The Pokémon jumped up and down, trying to free itself, but it was stuck fast. Ash knew this was it. "Now, Cyndaquil. Tackle!"

Cyndaquil was still shooting up toward the treetops. Quickly, it reversed its direction. It dove at Sandslash's head. Direct hit!

The force wrenched Sandslash's claw from the tree trunk. The Pokémon was free, but it was too stunned to battle. It wobbled back and forth a few times. Then it fainted.

"You did it!" Ash shouted.

"Cyndaquil wins," Brock declared.

"That was great!" Misty said.

"*Pika!*"

"*Togi!*"

The Pokémon added their congratulations.

But the boy wasn't big on fighting fair. He grabbed a net and began chasing Cyndaquil. "I'll get that Pokémon!"

Ash couldn't believe it. "That's cheating," he protested.

The boy glowered at Ash. He took another swipe at Cyndaquil with the net.

"Cyynnndaaa!" Cyndaquil was finally ready to use its Flamethrower. It blasted the other Trainer with a river of fire.

"Aaaahhhh!" the boy's clothes were smoking as he ran screaming into the forest.

"That's what you get for cheating!" Misty called after him.

"Good job, Cyndaquil," Ash praised it.

"You earned that Pokémon," Brock told Ash.

"Yeah, good job," Misty said.

Ash looked down at Cyndaquil. "I'll be counting on you a lot."

Ash thought about his other Fire-type Pokémon – Charizard. He had learned a lot while training Charizard. He was going to use what he'd learned to help

Cyndaquil grow into a strong Pokémon. *I'm going to do my best to train this Pokémon right!*

"Come on, everybody," he called to his friends. "I've got badges to earn!"

So Ash headed to Azalea Town with his confidence back — and a new Pokémon to call his own.

Next in this series:

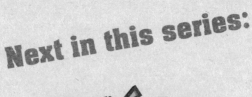

Team Rocket is rounding up Pokémon in the Johto region! They can't wait to get their greedy hands on Ledyba, Hoppip, and Wooper. It's up to Ash to protect these Pokémon – or so he thinks. These Pokémon have a plan of their own.